W9-BUD-002

CHICAGO PUBLIC LIBRARY
FORM 19

DISCARD

AMAZON ABC

BY KATHY DARLING

PHOTOGRAPHS BY TARA DARLING

Lothrop, Lee & Shepard Books New York

Acknowledgments

Thank you to Peter Jensen, whose Explorama Lodges in the heart of the Amazon near Iquitos, Peru, were our home during the winter of 1994. Without the wonderful trackers and guides there, we never would have gotten from A to Z.

We are particularly grateful to have been able to visit the Amazon Center for Environmental Education and Research (ACEER), with its unique walkway at the top of the canopy. Special thanks to managers Paul Donahue and Theresa Wood for helping us with bird identification.

Inquiries should be addressed to Lothrop, Lee & Shepard Books, a division of William Morrow & Company, Inc., 1350 Avenue of the Americas, New York, New York 10019.
Printed in Singapore
First Edition 1 2 3 4 5 6 7 8 9 10
Library of Congress Cataloging in Publication Data
Darling, Kathy.
Amazon A B C / by Kathy Darling; photographs by Tara Darling.
p. cm.
Summary: Labeled photographs present an alphabet of Amazonian animals, from the agouti to the zorillo.
ISBN 0-688-13778-4.— ISBN 0-688-13779-2 (lib. bdg.)
1. Zoology—Amazon River Region—Pictorial works—Juvenile literature. 2. English language—Alphabet—Juvenile literature.
[1. Zoology—Amazon River Region. 2. Alphabet.] I. Darling, Tara, ill. II. Title. QL235.D3 1996 591.981'1'0222—dc20
95-23114 CIP AC

UNITED STATES

AMAZON RAIN FOREST

THE AMAZING AMAZON

The most amazing thing about the Amazon rain forest is its size. Imagine, if you can, a green canopy of trees so vast that almost the entire United States could fit beneath its shade. This rain forest is bigger than all the other rain forests in the world combined.

The Amazon is the most alive place on earth. Ninety percent of the earth's five million *known* species of plants and animals are found there, and scientists think there may be as many as eighty million more species in the Amazon that haven't yet been identified. Fewer than one percent of all the Amazon's plants and animals have been studied.

This book will show you some of the wondrous animals to be found in the green treasure house we call the Amazon.

agouti (ah-GOOT-ee)

Bb

butterfly

capybara (cap-ee-BAR-uh)

Dd

damselfly

Ee

egret

frog

grasshopper

hoatzin (wha-TSEEN)

Ii

iguana

Jj

jacana (juh-KHAN-uh)

Kk

katydid

leaf-cutting ant

marmoset

Nn

nun bird

Oo

oropendola (or-oh-PEN-doh-luh)

Pp

parrot

quan (kwahn)

Rr

red-tailed boa

sloth

Tt

tapir

urania moth

vine snake

walking stick

Xx

x-ray fish

yellow-ridged toucan

zorillo (zor-EE-oh)

THE THREE WORLDS OF THE RAIN FOREST

At the top of the Amazon rain forest is the **canopy**. Here the crowns of giant trees, more than a hundred feet above the ground, are thick with leaves, flowers, and fruit. Most rain-forest animals live in the sunny canopy, feasting on the abundant food. The canopy dwellers live in a world that is light, hot, wet, and windy.

Below the canopy is the **understory**. Bushes, shrubs, vines, and small trees fight for the patches of sunlight that filter through the canopy. There is food and shelter here for small and medium-sized animals.

The bottom of the rain forest is called the **forest floor**. The Amazon doesn't qualify as a jungle because jungles have a tangle of vegetation at ground level. The Amazon floor is surprisingly open. Only one percent of the sunlight reaches the ground, so very few plants can live there. The air is still and the humidity high, but many large animals are able to make a living in this gloomy green twilight world.

ABOUT THE ANIMALS

Agouti (ah-GOOT-ee)
Agoutis are rodents that search the forest floor for seeds and nuts that drop from the canopy. Their sharp front teeth are strong enough to crack a Brazil nut, and their cheek pouches are big enough to carry a dozen nuts back to the nest.

Butterfly
The color of a butterfly tells you where it lives in the rain forest. Orange and blue butterflies fly openly in the bright sunlight of the canopy. These colors, a warning of poison, are meant to be seen. Butterflies with stripes and spots are found in the understory. Their patterns blend in with the patches of sun and shadow. Glasswings and other see-through butterflies rarely leave the dark forest floor, where they are almost invisible.

Capybara (cap-ee-BAR-uh)
The capybara is the world's largest rodent, weighing up to two hundred pounds. Webbed feet with hooflike nails help this giant plant-eating relative of the guinea pig get around in the muddy swamps of the Amazon.

Damselfly
Damselflies are relatives of dragonflies. These insect eaters live in the understory and on the forest floor. A good way to tell the two insect families apart is to check the position of the wings. Damselflies fold their four wings over their backs when they are resting. Dragonflies leave them open.

Egret
There are several kinds of egrets in the Amazon. Most eat fish, but buff-backed herons, commonly known as cattle egrets, eat insects. Amazon egrets do not migrate, as many other birds do, because there is a year-round source of food for them in the understory and on the forest floor.

Frog
Frogs in the Amazon don't need a pond because the tropical air at all levels of the rain forest is so heavy with moisture that their skin doesn't dry out. The insect eaters in these photos are all tree frogs. They climb with the help of glue that oozes onto flattened disks on the ends of their toes.

Brightly colored poison dart frogs live on the forest floor, but they climb up to the canopy to raise their tadpoles in trapped pools of water. They are small enough to fit on a dime.

These green and brown frogs have no poison. They depend on darkness and camouflage colors for protection. Sometimes called laughing frogs, their chickenlike cackling rings out from medium-sized bushes and small trees through the night.

Grasshopper
There are over twenty thousand species of grasshoppers. Many of those in the Amazon are brightly colored. The special color combinations help them identify others of their own kind, as do unique songs and dances. They live in the grass and small bushes close to the forest floor.

Hoatzin (wha-TSEEN)
The prehistoric-looking hoatzins are the only flying animals that eat only leaves. People call them stinkbirds because of their odor, which is caused by bacteria that help digest their food. They live in the understory.

Iguana
Green iguanas are leaping lizards. These vegetarian reptiles, which look fiercer than they really are, sun themselves on tree branches in the understory. When they are frightened, they leap off—sometimes right onto what they were trying to avoid.

Jacana (juh-KHAN-uh)
Very long toes and four-inch toenails enable this water-dwelling eater of plants and small animals to walk on floating weeds. The father jacana tends a nest among the lily pads and watches over the baby birds until they are big enough to follow in his footsteps.

Katydid
You can tell katydids from grasshoppers by their long antennas. Some species are very fierce. The horned katydid in the lower right photo belongs to a group called the coneheads.

Some katydids look like leaves. The upper left photo shows one with fake rot spots and mock insect nibbles. This species is easily mistaken for part of one of the understory plants on which katydids live.

Leaf-cutting ant
There are more ants in the rain forest than all other animals combined, and there are more leaf cutters than any other kind of ant. These hard-working gardeners live below the forest floor in giant nests that may contain a billion individuals. The ants do not eat the bits of leaf that they carry to the nest. The leaves are used to make food in an underground fungus garden.

Marmoset

Pygmy marmosets are sap suckers. They cling with sharp claws to tree trunks and chew out holes so they can lap up the sugary syrup that gathers. By far the smallest monkey, pygmies weigh less than most candy bars.

Nun bird

Nun birds are easier to watch than most rain forest birds because they nest in holes in the ground. Like other puff-birds, they are also easy to watch because they are curious. Nun birds will sit for hours watching you watch them.

Oropendola (or-oh-PEN-doh-luh)

These fruit-eating tropical members of the oriole family make sock-shaped nests in the understory, next to the hives of wasps or biting bees. Oropendolas use the hive dwellers as guards. The aggressive insects come to accept the birds but sting any would-be egg robbers.

Parrot

Parrots are big showoffs. You can't miss their brilliant colors or earsplitting shrieks. Wild parrots live in flocks high in the canopy. They are ace fliers and acrobatic climbers. When they climb, they use both their feet, which are specialized for grasping, and their great hooked beaks.

Parrots seem to have a favored foot, the way people have a favored hand. The yellow-headed Amazon in the lower left photo is obviously a left-footed parrot. The other parrots are, clockwise, a blue-and-gold macaw, a festive parrot, and scarlet macaws.

Quan (kwahn)

The plump quan, more often called the guan or jungle turkey, isn't a very good flier, and no amount of practice seems to help. Within an hour of hatching, this bird flies as well as it ever will. It lives in the understory, where it eats fruits and seeds.

Red-tailed boa

The meat-eating constrictors are the largest snakes in the world. They kill their prey not with poison, but by coiling around the animal and suffocating it. Red-tailed boas hunt at night, using heat-sensitive pits on their lips to locate animals sleeping in the trees. Found at all levels of the rain forest, they can afford to be very patient hunters—one meal can last an entire year!

Sloth

Even though the Amazon rain forest is always hot, the three-toed sloth is wrapped in a furry coat. Its low-calorie diet of canopy leaves doesn't provide enough energy to keep the sloth warm. The sloth is the slowest land animal in the world and does everything at an unhurried pace in order to conserve energy. It blinks slowly and even sneezes in slow motion.

Tapir

A baby tapir is striped and spotted, but it will be solid brown by the time it grows up. The tapir uses its long nose to grasp the leaves it eats from bushes along the forest floor in the same way an elephant uses its much longer trunk.

Urania moth

More brilliantly colored than most butterflies, urania moths fly through the understory in the daytime. Their wings, which appear green in the photo, are made of reflecting scales that appear blue or yellow when viewed from different angles.

Vine snake

The nonpoisonous vine snake lives in the understory. It likes to hide in heliconia plants because water collects in the flowers and attracts birds and frogs, which the snake likes to eat.

Walking stick

Walking sticks are vegetarians and belong to a group of insects whose natural body shape camouflages them. They also have the ability to change color to match a plant and can stand motionless on a bush in the understory for hours on end to avoid detection.

X-ray fish

X-ray fish have skin as clear as glass. You can see their insides right through it. Although these popular aquarium fish are only two inches long, they have the same appetite for meat as their bigger relatives, the dreaded piranhas.

Yellow-ridged toucan

The toucan's huge bill looks heavy, but the hard shell is a thin covering over honeycombed bone that gives it strength without weight. It lives in the canopy, where it eats fruits and seeds.

Zorillo (zor-EE-oh)

This meat- and insect-eating rodent look-alike is a marsupial related to the kangaroo. A newborn zorillo is no larger than a grain of rice. Zorillos live in the understory and on the forest floor.